SHABANU: DAUGHTER OF THE WIND

by
Suzanne Fisher Staples

Teacher Guide

Written by
Elizabeth Klar
Cheryl Klar-Trim

· Note

The Knopf Paperback edition of the book published by Alfred A. Knopf, Inc., ©1989 by Suzannne Fisher Staples, was used to prepare this guide. The page references may differ in the hardcover or other paperback editions.

Please note: Please assess the appropriateness of this book for the age level and maturity of your students prior to reading and discussing it with your class.

ISBN 1-58130-632-6

To order, contact your local school supply store, or—

Novel Units, Inc.
P.O. Box 97
Bulverde, TX 78163-0097

Web site: www.educyberstor.com

Table of Contents

Skills and Strategies

Thinking
Identifying attributes,
compare/contrast,
pros/cons, brainstorming,
research, problem solving

Comprehension
Predicting, sequencing,
summarization, cause/effect,
inference, main idea

Writing
Character journal, personal
writing, eulogy, poetry, ode,
parts of speech

Vocabulary
Target words, context clues,
root/base words,
synonym/antonym, word
maps, charades

Listening/Speaking
Dramatizing, interviewing,
discussion, music,
story-telling

Literary Elements
Characterization, setting,
plot development

Across the Curriculum
Social Studies—maps, family
tree, culture/customs,
religion; Science/Health
Issues—safety, sensory;
Astronomy; Geography;
Research; Art—drawing,
collage, design and color,
body painting;
Music—chants, songs,
lute music

Summary

Shabanu is the story of a young Pakistani girl who lives in the Cholistan Desert. Shabanu is one of two daughters in a family with no sons. Being the youngest, she is allowed to care for the camels and does not have to work in the house. She is a strong-willed girl who loves her freedom, the desert, and her camels.

According to tradition, the older daughter, Phulan, has been promised in marriage to Hamir, and Shabanu is promised to his brother, Murad. While preparing for Phulan's coming wedding, tragedy strikes as the two sisters are fetching water at the nearby canal. When they confront a powerful and cruel landowner, Hamir is killed. As a result, Phulan must now marry Murad, the man Shabanu loves, and Shabanu must make a great sacrifice in order to appease the wealthy landowner. She must choose between upholding the honor of her family by marrying a man with three other wives or seeking her own freedom in the desert.

About the Author

Suzanne Fisher Staples lives in New York City. She has served as a UPI correspondent in Asia, Hong Kong, Pakistan, Afghanistan, India, and Washington, D.C. While she was working in Pakistan, she associated with the nomads of the Cholistan Desert. Suzanne used her knowledge of the desert people to write her first book, *Shabanu*. She has also written a sequel to *Shabanu* titled *Haveli* and a her third book, *Dangerous Skies*.

Introductory Activities

1. **Previewing the book:** Have students look at the book and answer the journalist's questions about what they see: who? what? where? when? why? Based on their answers, students predict what the book will be about.

2. Given the following clues, students write a paragraph predicting what they think will happen in the story.

   tradition   honor   daughters   father   obey   sacrifice

3. **Character Journal:** List the main characters from *Shabanu* and have the students choose one. As they read the book, students write regular journal entries from that character's point of view. Journal entries should reflect on the events of the story. At various points in their reading, have the students share their journal entries with classmates.

4. Create an attribute web (see next page) with students for each of the following ideas: Family, freedom, heritage, home, culture. Focus one word at a time. Begin by writing the word in the center of a large piece of paper. Ask students to quickly tell what each word brings to mind. Encourage students to elaborate on particular ideas.

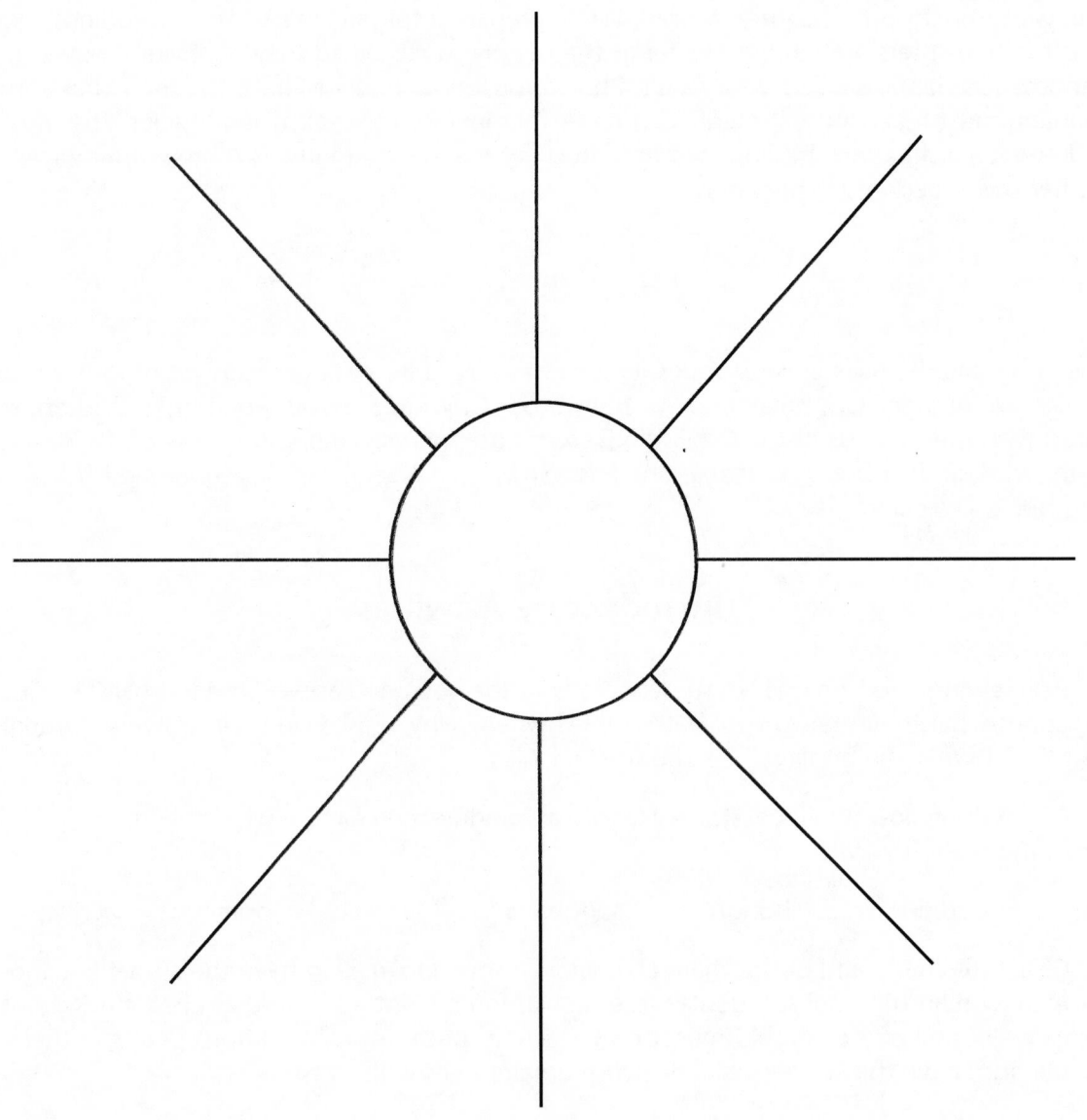

5. **Prediction Chart:** Have students set up a prediction chart (see pages 7-8 of this guide) to use as they read the book.

6. **Anticipation Questions:** Have students respond to each of the following statements with a "thumbs-up" (I agree) or a "thumbs-down" (I disagree) and discuss their responses.

> *Children should always obey their parents.*
> *It's important to follow the traditions of your culture.*
> *Young adults should have a say in their future.*
> *Arranged marriages are necessary and right.*
> *Everyone should have the option to make all their own choices.*

7. **Social Studies:** Have students prepare a family tree. They should include members of their immediate family and their extended family as far as their records can go. Students should list the city or country where the family member lives. Students should list all of the nationalities that represent the members of their families.

8. Have students read the names of the characters that appear at the beginning of the book. Then have them look at the map of Pakistan and the inset in order to familiarize themselves with the country in which the characters live.

9. A glossary at the end of the book will explain unfamiliar words used in the story. Students should study and discuss these words in class.

Vocabulary Activities

1. **Target Word Charades:** Have students act out some of the vocabulary words while classmates guess the target word. Some suggested words for *Shabanu*:

sloshing (12)	fodder (48)	mute (62)	waddles (78)
obsessed (106)	protrude (135)	splutters (156)	pelting (175)
wisps (200)	wits (227)		

2. **Target Word Maps:** Have students complete word maps for vocabulary words of a certain part of speech. For example, *verbs* from *Shabanu* would include:

irritated (4)   prowling (13)   consumed (32)   plops (49)
stoop (79)   intertwine (105)   clamor (125)   dawdling (145)
appease (163)   reeling (193)

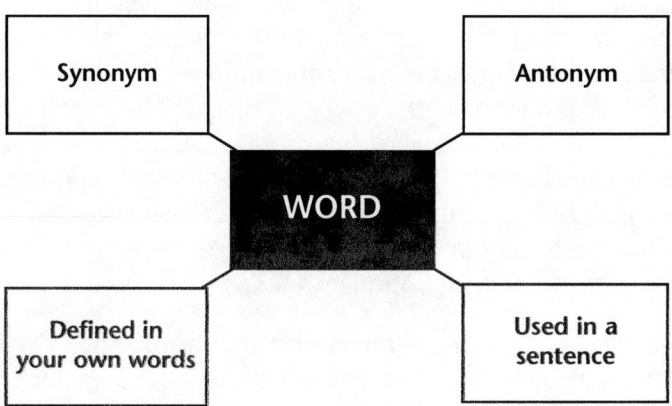

3. **Sentences:** Have students select five or six vocabulary words and use as many of the words as possible in one sentence. Students should complete at least five sentences. Have the students share their sentences with a partner.

4. **Synonym Match:** Have students select vocabulary words from a chapter and list one synonym for each vocabulary word on a small piece of paper. Students mix the papers and match each synonym to the appropriate vocabulary word.

5. **Root/Base Words:** Have students find the base or root word for at least eight vocabulary words. Students look at each word and answer the following questions: What is the meaning of the root word? What is the meaning of the vocabulary word? What prefix or suffix has been added to the vocabulary word? What is the meaning of the prefix or suffix? How has the meaning of the root/base word changed by adding the prefix or suffix?

6. **Vocabulary Sort:** Have students sort vocabulary words into categories (e.g., nouns, verbs, and adjectives/adverbs).

7. **Odd One Out:** Use vocabulary words from one or two chapters. Make a chain of words. One word in the chain is the vocabulary word, two words are synonyms for the vocabulary word, and one word does not go with the others. (Mix the sequence of the words in the chain.) Students must circle the word that does not belong with the others and explain how it differs.

Using Predictions in the Novel Unit Approach

We all make predictions as we read—little guesses about what will happen next, how a conflict will be resolved, which details will be important to the plot, which details will help fill in our sense of a character. Students should be encouraged to predict, to make sensible guesses as they read the novel.

As students work on their predictions, these discussion questions can be used to guide them: What are some of the ways to predict? What is the process of a sophisticated reader's thinking and predicting? What clues does an author give to help us make predictions? Why are some predictions more likely to be accurate than others?

Create a chart for recording predictions. This could be either an individual or class activity. As each subsequent chapter is discussed, students can review and correct their previous predictions about plot and characters as necessary.

Use the facts and ideas the author gives.

Use your own prior knowledge.

Apply any new information (i.e., from class discussion) that may cause you to change your mind.

Predictions:

_____

_____

_____

_____

Prediction Chart

What characters have we met so far?	What is the conflict in the story?	What are your predictions?	Why did you make those predictions?

Using Character Webs in the Novel Unit Approach

Attribute webs are simply a visual representation of a character from the novel. They provide a systematic way for students to organize and recap the information they have about a particular character. Attribute webs may be used after reading the novel to recapitulate information about a particular character, or completed gradually as information unfolds. They may be completed individually or as a group project.

One type of character attribute web uses these divisions:

- How a character acts and feels. (How does the character act? How do you think the character feels? How would you feel if this happened to you?)

- How a character looks. (Close your eyes and picture the character. Describe him/her to me.)

- Where a character lives. (Where and when does the character live?)

- How others feel about the character. (How does another specific character feel about our character?)

In group discussion about the characters described in student attribute webs, the teacher can ask for backup proof from the novel. Inferential thinking can be included in the discussion.

Attribute webs need not be confined to characters. They may also be used to organize information about a concept, object, or place.

Attribute Web

The attribute web below will help you gather clues the author provides about a character in the novel. Fill in the blanks with words and phrases which tell how the character acts and looks, as well as what the character says and what others say about him or her.

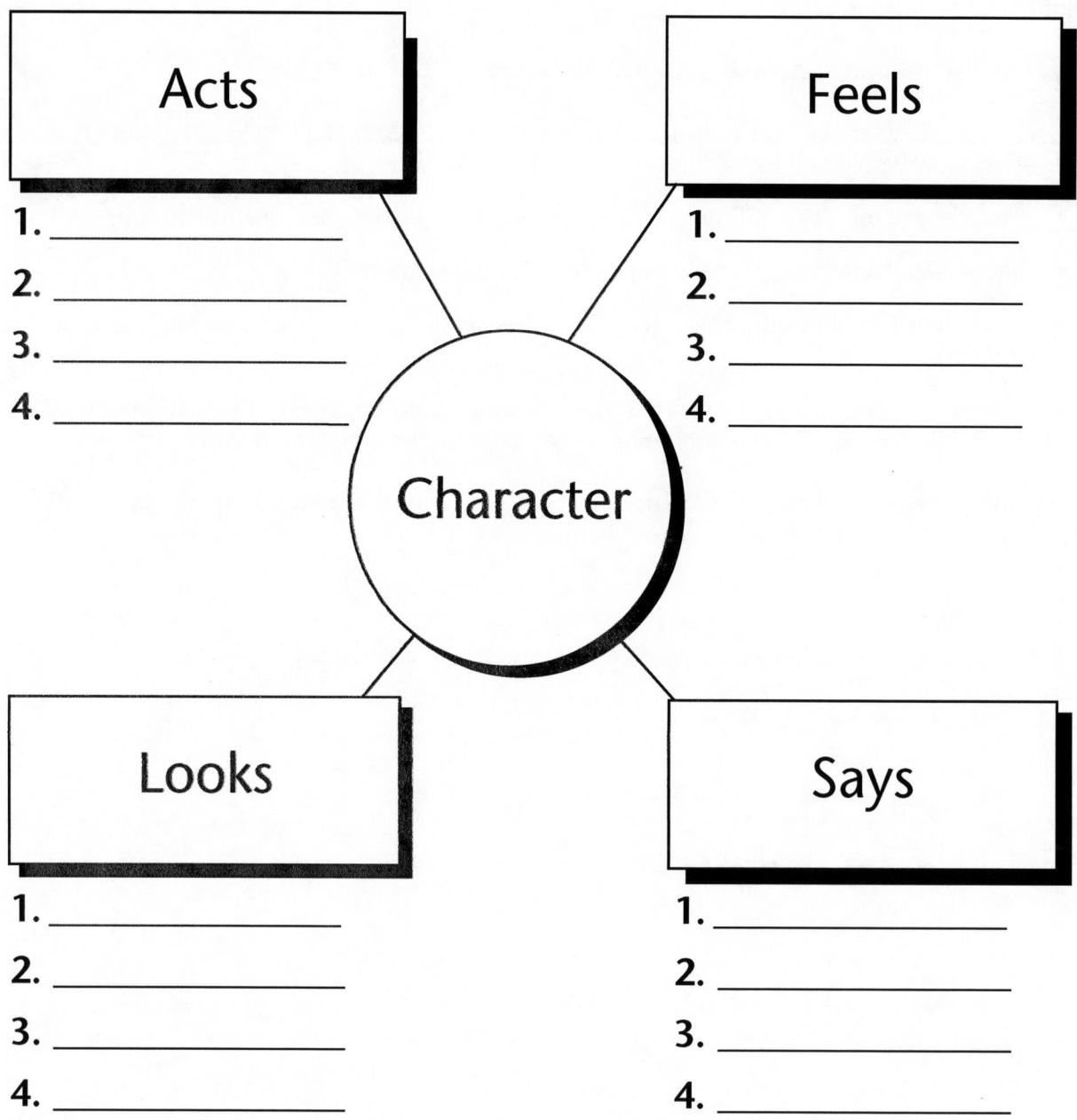

Story Map

Characters_____

_____

Time and Place_____

_____

Problem_____

_____

_____

Goal_____

_____

_____

Beginning ⟶ Development ⟶ Outcome

_____

_____

_____

_____

Resolution_____

_____

_____

_____

_____

Setting

Problem

Goal

Episodes

Resolution

Part 1—
Guluband, pages 1-12 and Birth, pages 13-19

Vocabulary
Guluband—

hazed (2)	shuffling (2)	thatched (2)	turban (2)
opal (2)	kneads (3)	dowries (3)	pudgy (3)
purses (3)	sapphire (4)	irritated (4)	parch (4)
dunes (5)	disheveled (5)	betrothal (5)	tunic (5)
fragile (6)	unimaginable (6)	splatters (7)	darts (7)
harnesses (7)	giddy (7)	lurches (10)	swivel (10)
nimble (11)	quench (12)	sloshing (12)	

Birth—

prowling (13)	bellow (14)	spiky (14)	swarming (14)
disembowel (14)	rigid (15)	krait (15)	tumbles (15)
paralyzed (15)	desperation (15)	mucus (15)	fetching (15)
shuttered (15)	splayed (15)	perched (15)	inert (16)
foster (16)	inevitable (16)	wail (16)	twitch (16)
flutter (16)	bleating (16)	carcass (16)	gurgling (16)
briskly (17)	nuzzles (17)	organize (17)	trembly (17)
nudges (17)	gingerly (17)	billowy (18)	jumble (18)
yearling (19)	weaned (19)		

Discussion Questions

1. Why are Phulan and Shabanu scared by the thoughts of marrying Hamir and Murad? *(Hamir and Murad's people have strange customs and have accused Shabanu's family of stealing.)*

2. Why is Mama sewing new dresses for Phulan? *(Phulan is going to be married.)*

3. Why do you think Shabanu and Phulan are happy when it rains? *(Answers will vary.)*

4. What would have happened to the family if it had not rained? *(They would have moved to Dingarh.)*

5. What does Mama mean when she says, "There is no such thing as too much water"? *(Answers will vary.)*

6. How does Shabanu know she should push on the camel's stomach to help deliver the baby camel? *(Shabanu remembers her mother pushed on Auntie's stomach to help in the delivery of her cousins.)*

7. Why do you think Shabanu tries so hard to save the baby camel? *(Answers will vary.)*

8. What makes Shabanu think that a snake bit the mother camel? *(Shabanu sees two puncture marks on the camels nose. She also knows that rain forces snakes out above ground.)*

9. Why is Shabanu's father upset about losing the mother camel? *(The camel and baby were supposed to be part of Phulan's dowry.)*

Supplementary Activities

1. **Geography:** Have students locate Pakistan, Afghanistan, and India in a world atlas. The students should answer the following questions: In what hemisphere does Pakistan lie? Between what latitudes and longitudes does Pakistan lie? About how many miles is Pakistan from where you live? How many square miles does Pakistan encompass? What kinds of landforms are in Pakistan? What are the names of major rivers and deserts there? (Note: Alternate Pakistan with Afghanistan and India for additional geography activities.)

2. **Research:** Have students consult reference books for answers to the following questions: What in the current population of Pakistan? What are the major cities of Pakistan? What are the major industries of Pakistan? What languages are spoken in Pakistan? What religions are practiced in Pakistan? What type of clothing do the Pakistanis wear? (Note: Alternate Pakistan with Afghanistan then India for additional research activitities.)

3. **Critical Thinking:** Have students create a T-chart that lists the positive and negative things about living with extended family (aunts, uncles, cousins, and/or grandparents).

Positive	Negative

4. **Literary Analysis/Character:** Have students begin a character attribute web (see pages 9-10 of this guide) for each sister. Students should continue to add information to the web as they read the chapters.

5. **Literary Analysis/Story Maps:** Have students begin a story map (see page 11 of this guide) to use as they read the story. As they go through the book, they should continue to add new information about the characters, setting, problems, and events of the story.

Part 2—
Kalu, 20-30; Safari, pages 31-40 and The Bugtis, pages 41-46

Vocabulary

Kalu—

curds (22)	fancies(22)	haunches (22)	strenuous (22)
slobbering (22)	belch (22)	shies (22)	insistently (22)
lopes (22)	dominant (23)	suppress (23)	ardor (23)
scramble (23)	deft (24)	feint (24)	foreleg (24)
enraged (24)	obsessed (24)	thwacking (24)	heave (24)
angling (24)	reverberating (24)	thrash (24)	slash (25)
dignity (25)	diverted (25)	stave (25)	unwinding (25)
lunges (25)	domed (25)	bolt (26)	gamboling (26)
pestles (26)	venting (26)	wrath (26)	absorbed (26)
twines (26)	glistening (26)	flailing (27)	veering (27)
approximately (27)	jangles (27)	hobbling (27)	lentils (28)
languid (29)	status (29)	skids (29)	abide (29)
smoldering (30)	fetch (30)	vengeance (30)	

Safari—

glimmer (31)	tassels (31)	bangles (31)	flanks (32)
whorls (32)	chevrons (32)	henna (32)	malevolent (32)
grudge (32)	panniers (32)	udders (32)	mesh (32)
consumed (32)	plaited (33)	spiraling (33)	perpendicular (34)
opalescent (34)	knave (34)	shimmer (34)	mirage (34)
pace (34)	lulls (34)	rubble (35)	accumulated (35)
silhouette (35)	hemisphere (35)	squats (35)	redistribute (35)
flickers (35)	tunics (36)	berets (36)	whisk (36)
mange (37)	towers (37)	rupees (37)	deferential (37)
shrugging (37)	illuminate (38)	intensity (38)	infinite (38)
mosque (38)	sagging (38)	consorts (38)	tethered (39)
latticed (39)	balustrades (39)	intricate (39)	Koran (39)
bullock (39)	acrid (40)	dung (40)	clink (40)

The Bugtis—

seething (42)	pediments (42)	stand (42)	sinewy (42)
filigree (42)	hospitable (42)	loom (43)	jolting (43)
voluminous (43)	bandoliers (43)	export (45)	thrashing (45)
unbearable (45)	numb (45)		

Discussion Questions

1. How do you think Shabanu feels about Mama making her a new long skirt and dress, Shabanu's first grown-up clothes? *(Answers will vary.)*

2. How are Muslim girls brought up to think about their homes? *(They are brought up to believe that their childhood homes are only temporary and their real homes are the ones they go to when they marry.)*

3. Why do Tipu and Kalu fight? *(They fight for dominance over the herd.)*

4. Why do Dadi, Shabanu, and Phulan try to separate the fighting camels? *(The camels will fight to the death and the family does not want to lose either camel.)*

5. Why doesn't Shabanu want to leave Mithoo behind as she, Phulan, and Dadi escape from the angry camel? *(She is afraid the other camels will push him away and he'll be scared.)*

6. Why do you think Mama says Shabanu must learn to obey or else she is afraid for her? *(Answers will vary.)*

7. How does Shabanu feel about having to obey Murad when they marry? *(Answers will vary.)*

8. What does Shabanu mean as she reflects that men are not so different from camels? *(Neither leaves an old argument unsettled.)*

9. Why do Auntie and Mama tell Shabanu to wear a *chadr*? *(Auntie says a young lady should not go with her head uncovered. Mama says it will keep the sun off Shabanu's head.)*

10. How do you believe Shabanu feels when she thinks Dadi is going to sell Guluban to the desert rangers? *(Answers will vary.)*

11. Why does Dadi tell Shabanu that the Bugtis will kill the daughter who eloped as soon as they find her? *(He is reminding Shabanu of the consequences of not being obedient.)*

Supplementary Activities

1. **Literary Analysis/Character:** Have students discuss the differences and similarities between Dadi and Mama. Students then make a Venn diagram that shows how the two parents are alike and how they are different.

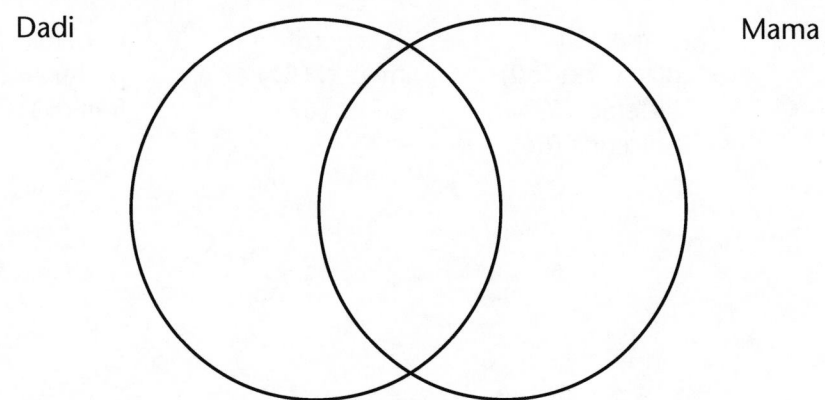

Dadi   Mama

2. **Research:** Have the students do some research to answer the following questions: How many types of camels are there? Where are most camels found in the world? What are the main uses of camels? What kinds of food do camels eat? What are some interesting facts about camels (list at least three)?

3. **Writing:** Phulan is now old enough to marry. A Muslim girl is brought up knowing her childhood home is only temporary. Her real home is the one that is decided upon by her father when he chooses the husband for his daughter. Discuss what you think about this custom? Write a short composition about how a father might decide on the husband for his daughter.

4. **Art:** Have each of the students draw a camel and decorate it according to the description in the Safari chapter. The students should work together to illustrate a background of the desert. Have the students place the camels on the background to simulate Shabanu's trip to Sibi. Display the picture in the room.

5. **Poetry:** On the way to Sibi, Shabanu and her father sing songs about their trip and what they will buy and sell. Have the students make up a poem about a trip to town and what they will buy. Have students share their poems.

Part 3—
Sibi Fair, pages 47-56 and The Bargain, pages 57-64

Vocabulary

Sibi Fair—

engulfed (48)	bullocks (48)	garlanded (48)	haggle (48)
fodder (48)	fringed (48)	tangy (48)	excrement (48)
rut (48)	plops (49)	defines (49)	reed (49)
pries (49)	booty (49)	prospective (50)	daredevil (50)
pipe organ (50)	scaffolding (51)	plummet (51)	betel (52)
demurely (52)	withered (52)	flutters (52)	peer (52)
gravelly (52)	deformed (53)	undulating (53)	immobile (53)
sinister (54)	kilos (55)	vendor (55)	compassion (56)

The Bargain—

companionable (57)	curry (59)	scurry (59)	tarpaulin (60)
ruminate (60)	plastering (60)	riveted (61)	patter (62)
mute (62)	tattered (63)	glints (63)	frail (63)
mutton (64)	portends (64)		

Discussion Questions

1. How does Dadi respond when Shabanu asks if he was scared of the Bugtis? *(He says he felt Allah willed them to be safe.)*

2. What do you think Shabanu wants to happen or not happen when she asks her father, "Do you think if you believe something hard enough, it will happen?" *(Answers will vary.)*

3. Why do you think there are no women at the Sibi Fair, just young girls Shabanu's age and younger? *(Answers will vary.)*

4. How do you think Shabanu feels as she rides Guluban through the streets at the Sibi Fair and everyone looks at them thinking what a fine animal Guluban is? *(Answers will vary.)*

5. Why does Shabanu refer to the person who serves her the paan as a "man-woman"? *(She was dressed like a woman, but had facial hair and a deep voice.)*

6. Why does Dadi ask the Afghans to pay twice as much for the herd as the other buyers? *(He does not want them to buy the herd.)*

7. Why does Shabanu decide that she can't run away with Guluban? *(There is no place a girl can go by herself safely, she knows no one outside of her family, and she has no money.)*

8. Why does the man from Zhob feel he receives a good bargain for Dadi's camels? *(Answers will vary.)*

9. How does Shabanu feel about Dadi selling Guluband? *(She feels her joy, her freedom, and all of who she is has gone.)*

10. How will the sale of the camels help Shabanu's family? *(It will pay for Phulan and Shabanu's dowries and give Mama and Dadi a better life.)*

Supplementary Activities

1. **Writing:** Shabanu has many chores on the way to the Sibi Carnival. Have the students pretend to be Shabanu and write their thoughts beginning with the following sentences: I must make our camp. It will be hours before I can slip away to the carnival. He lifts me to his shoulders so I can see everything, and we walk through the fairgrounds.

2. **Critical Thinking:** Shabanu lives in a tent without electricity or running water. Have students list ten ways their lives would change if their homes had no electricity.

3. **Creative Thinking:** Dadi and Mama do not own a television. Have students list ways they could entertain themselves if they did not have a television.

4. **Discussion:** How do you think Shabanu feels when she finds out that Dadi has sold her favorite camel? How do you think Dadi feels when he must sell Shabanu's favorite camel?

Part 4—
Shatoosh, pages 65-76 and Dowry, pages 77-83

Vocabulary
Shatoosh—

pulses (66)	staccato (66)	mesmerized (66)	sag (67)
defeats (68)	monotonous (68)	shuffle (68)	incident (69)
crook (70)	husky (70)	tumbles(70)	stark (70)
detached (70)	alien (70)	bazaar (70)	prickly (70)
polyester (70)	outrageous (71)	crinkled (71)	trellises (71)
gnarled (72)	wispy (72)	gossamer (73)	fawn (73)
shimmers (74)	shroud (75)	dignified (75)	pulse (75)
symphony (76)	muffled (76)		

Dowry—

fiercely (77)	pretensions (78)	insinuating (78)	waddles (78)
thumping (78)	unlashes (78)	fond (78)	stoop (79)
animation (80)	grieve (80)	penetrate (80)	fluid (81)
mesh (81)	gambols (81)	nimble (82)	jolts (82)
slaughtered (82)	exclaims (82)	creases (82)	sprawl (83)
twine (83)			

Discussion Questions

1. How do the men behave at Dadi's camp as they celebrate? *(They dance and sing and share food.)*

2. Why doesn't Shabanu want to carry the puppy Dadi gives her? *(She is too exhausted.)*

3. Why does Dadi insist that Shabanu ride on the camel as they pass through the Bugtis' land? *(He wants passers by to think they are a simple family returning from the Sibi Fair.)*

4. Why does Shabanu think that Lion Heart is a good name for the puppy? *(The puppy is strong and unafraid.)*

5. Why does the shopkeeper smile when Shabanu tells him her name? *(The shopkeeper's mother was also named Shabanu.)*

6. Why do you think the shopkeeper gives Shabanu his mother's shatoosh? *(Answers will vary.)*

7. How do you think Shabanu feels when the shopkeeper tells Dadi that she really is a princess? *(Answers will vary.)*

8. What does Mama mean when she says they'll have to keep an eye on Sher Dil every moment when they are at the settled area? *(The last time they were there, someone poisoned their dog.)*

9. How does Shabanu's family comfort her as she grieves for Guluband? *(Answers will vary.)*

10. How do you think Phulan feels about the items Dadi brings her for her dowry? *(Answers will vary.)*

Supplementary Activities

1. **Drama:** Have the students act out the scene where Shabanu receives the puppy from Dadi.

2. **Creative Thinking:** Have the students list names for Shabanu's puppy on the board. They should explain the reason for choosing the name. The class should then take a secret vote to choose their favorite two names for the puppy.

3. **Critical Thinking:** Shabanu searches for the perfect wedding gift for her sister, Phulan. Shabanu is a good sister. Have students create an attribute web (see page 34) which lists the qualities of a good sister. Display the attribute webs in the classroom.

4. **Science/Health:** Have the students invite a veterinarian to the class to discuss the proper care of a puppy.

Part 5—
Nose Pegs, pages 84-90 and Channan Pir, pages 91-102

Vocabulary

Nose Pegs—

bobs (85)	dwindling (85)	monsoon (85)	scum (85)
vague (86)	embankment (86)	trace (87)	spiteful (87)
juvenile (87)	tyrannical (88)	apprehensive (88)	fetlock (89)
hobbles (89)	thrashes (89)	smarting (90)	

Channan Pir—

pannier (92)	livery (92)	festooned (92)	medallions (92)
sequined (92)	disk (92)	khaki (93)	tunics (93)
billowing (93)	fez (93)	martial (93)	converted (93)
valiantly (94)	intertwined (94)	raja (94)	askew (94)
pursued (94)	infantry (94)	trek (95)	slatternly (95)
shimmers (95)	troupe (96)	camaraderie (96)	twitter (96)
eternal (96)	ocher (96)	disgrace (97)	frenzy (99)
dervishes (99)	anguish (99)	trance (99)	queue (99)
supplicant (99)	jostling (100)	loincloths (100)	ox yoke (100)
crouch (100)	hurtles (100)	levering (101)	immense (101)
ecstasy (101)	thrashes (101)	fury (101)	

Discussion Questions

1. What do you think Shabanu means when she reflects that she is learning to save her spirit for when it can be useful? *(Answers will vary.)*

2. Why does Shabanu believe that the Bugti girl and her lover have been found and killed? *(There is no where to hide in the desert.)*

3. What do you think Shabanu means by Auntie and Uncle's marriage being a good match for different reasons? *(Answers will vary.)*

4. How does Xhush Dil react to his nose peg? *(He thrashes in anger and throws Auntie and Dadi to the ground.)*

5. What do you think Shabanu means when she says nothing that Auntie wears shows her good points "which sometimes are hidden even from our hearts"? *(Answers will vary.)*

6. What does Grandfather talk about on the way to Channan Pir? *(His adventures in war and various historical events; most of which he is confused about.)*

7. Who was Kalu and why do you think Grandfather remembers him so fondly? *(The great camel Grandfather rode in a battle, answers will vary.)*

8. Why does Auntie think that Fatima is a double disgrace? *(Because she is already sixteen and unmarried and does not want to marry.)*

9. Why do you think Dadi and Mama think Sharma is wonderful? *(Answers will vary.)*

10. How do you think Shabanu feels when she sees her father wrestling? *(Answers will vary.)*

Supplementary Activities

1. **Speaking/Listening:** Have students interview an older family member and ask that person to tell them an important family story. Have students retell the story to their classmates.

2. **Research/History:** Have students research the history of Pakistan. They are to list at least 10 important events that have occurred between 2500 BC and the present time. The students should use this list to create a time line about Pakistan by writing the date of the event and then illustrate the event. (Butcher paper can be used to make the time lines.) Display the time lines in the classroom.

3. **Writing:** Shabanu describes the night as she travels to the shrine at Channan Pir. Have students write an ode to their favorite time of day. An ode is a poem that celebrates a poet's love or admiration for something or someone. In the traditional ode, a poet talks directly to the thing or person to express feelings.

Part 6—
Sharma, pages 103-108 and Desert Storm, pages 109-120

Vocabulary

Sharma—

whisks (103)	tuberoses (104)	sculpted (104)	lute (105)
prophecy (105)	trills (105)	cadences (105)	lilting (105)
sandalwood (106)	sentinel (107)	soothing (107)	portends (107)
jabber (107)	unidentifiable (107)	unscramble (107)	tweak (108)
prances (108)	sympathize (108)		

Desert Storm—

torpid (109)	monstrous (110)	wedge (110)	remarkable (112)
lee (112)	wisps (112)	swirling (112)	thatch (112)
suffocated (113)	whimper (114)	filters (114)	cascades (114)
parched (114)	caked (114)	quivery (115)	obscenity (115)
devastation (115)	wrought (115)	debris (117)	waxing (117)
spindles (117)	eerie (118)	apprehensive (118)	groggy (118)
fitful (118)	makeshift (118)	slumped (118)	twined (118)
articulated (119)	lapis (119)	vigil (120)	bustle (120)

Discussion Questions

1. Why is Phulan clasping and unclasping her hands in pleasure? *(Because Sharma is going to bring her jelabi-wallah to fry crispy, sugar-filled pretzels and Fatima will bring tuberoses to Phulan's wedding.)*

2. Why are the women horrified and delighted by the stories told by Sharma and Shabanu? *(Answers will vary.)*

3. How does Shabanu feel as she visits the shrine for the first time? *(She feels as if she is in communion with the saint: his presence seems to be like a soothing hand on her shoulder.)*

4. Why does Sharma think that Shabanu and Phulan are lucky? *(Because they have a good father who has seen to it that they will marry well.)*

5. Why do you think that Mama always takes Auntie's superior attitude in good humor? *(Answers will vary.)*

6. How do you think Shabanu feels as she is awakened during the monstrous sandstorm? *(Answers will vary.)*

7. Why do you think Grandfather left the house during the sandstorm? *(Answers will vary.)*

8. Why can't Shabanu and Dadi find Grandfather during the storm? *(The vicious wind slaps them with thousands of sand grains and their voices are lost in the violent noise of the wind.)*

9. Why can't Shabanu and her father find the toba? *(The storm has covered the water up with sand.)*

10. What does Shabanu find under the sand-covered lump at the foot of a hillock? How does she feel? *(She finds a black baby camel. Answers will vary. She may be sad that the baby camel died and/or she may be glad that the lump was not Grandfather.)*

11. Why does Dadi throw his head back and look at the sky saying softly "Allah," Allah" as tears streak his face? *(Answers will vary.)*

12. Why do Mama, Phulan, and Shabanu need to begin packing their belongings? *(Because there is no more water for the animals or the people.)*

13. How did Grandfather survive the terrible sandstorm? *(He huddled among the camels at Mujarawala Toba where the dunes are high which in turn gave him some protection from the wind.)*

Supplementary Activities

1. **Science/Health/Research:** Have the students research the types of food which are eaten by the Pakistani people. The students could sample tea that is mixed with milk and sugar, examine and taste lentils, cook or have a parent cook a bread made with whole wheat flour and water which is prepared in a skillet, or any other Pakistani food.

2. **Discussion:** Have the students discuss the difficulties families have when a beloved member of the family becomes ill.

3. **Drama:** Have the students act out the scene during the sandstorm when the family is searching for Grandfather.

4. **Writing:** What is Dadi probably thinking when he is searching for Grandfather during the sandstorm? Have the students pretend to be Dadi and write their thoughts from the time Dadi begins the search through when he brings Grandfather home on the camel.

Part 7—
The Thirsty Dead, pages 121-129 and Derawar, pages 130-140

Vocabulary

The Thirsty Dead—

gingerly (121)	emblem (122)	soothe (122)	Mecca (123)
syncopation (123)	shivery (123)	browse (123)	silvery (124)
parchment (124)	fluted (124)	scalding (124)	clamor (125)
desolate (125)	convulses (125)	chants (126)	shroud (126)
quench (126)	jackals (126)	sprawled (126)	pestilence (126)
nimbleness (127)	detached (127)	skidding (127)	defying (127)
burnish (127)	turrets (127)	vaulted (128)	minarets (128)
shrivel (128)			

Derawar—

embodies (131)	insignificant (131)	bulbous (132)	hobbles (132)
indistinct (132)	corrupting (133)	meager (133)	gnome (133)
scrappy (134)	glisten (134)	cobbled (134)	stoops (134)
protrude (135)	envisioned (135)	fertile (135)	solitary (136)
pilgrims (137)	withered (139)		

Discussion Questions

1. Why are Mama and Dadi being so careful with the water pots? *(Water is scarce because the sandstorm has destroyed the toba.)*

2. Why does Mama put Grandfather's fez on his head? How do Mama and Shabanu feel about Grandfather? *(Answers will vary.)*

3. Why is it a custom to never get onto the camels in front of the home? *(The desert people believe that they will never return if they do.)*

4. Why are Phulan and Shabanu afraid to find the person who owns the pale blue tattered turban? *(There is a legend of the thirsty dead which says if you find a thirsty man too late to save his life, he'll moan and clamor, his ghost following you the rest of your life.)*

5. How does Mama feel about Grandfather? *(She says that he was a strong and brave man who was also gentle. He always made her feel like she was his own daughter.)*

6. Why is Shabanu worried about the water at the edge of the settlement? *(The well at the edge of a settlement is least likely to have good water. Shabanu's family is so thirsty that they will drink even salty water.)*

7. Why do Shabanu and Dadi need to hurry to bury Grandfather? *(The heat of the day will be fierce and the body of Grandfather will begin to smell and swell up.)*

8. Why does Dadi begin to grow angry with Sulaiman, the keeper of the tombs? *(Because the stubborn old man wants to show his meager power by not allowing them to see the fort and tombs.)*

9. Why do Shabanu and her father ask only Shahzada to share their dinner? *(The village people are not friendly and Shahzada is the only helpful soul they find.)*

10. Why do you think Mama and Phulan never talk about how Phulan should behave toward Hamir's mother when the wedding is over and they are all living together? *(Answers will vary.)*

Supplementary Activities

1. **Research:** Grandfather wants to be buried in the graveyard among his brothers who fell in battle in the service of the nawab. Have the students research the national cemeteries of the United States. Where are some of them located? Who can be buried there? Do the students have a national cemetery near where they live?

2. **Music/Art:** The lute is an instrument that is played in Pakistan. Obtain recordings of music played on the lute. While the students listen to the music, have them illustrate the images they get in their minds.

3. **Writing:** Have the students pretend that they are Shabanu and have them write their thoughts about Grandfather's death and how she feels about him dying.

Part 8—
Ramadan, pages 141-150 and The Landlord, 151-160

Vocabulary
Ramadan—

stanchion (142)	pallid (143)	felled (143)	shimmering (143)
pendulous (144)	ladle (145)	noble (146)	browsing (147)
compensation (147)	influencing (148)	sickles (148)	rafters (149)
jasmine (149)	deft (149)	appendages (149)	anemic (150)
twinge (150)			

The Landlord—

lathered (152)	sheen (153)	elaborately (153)	manicured (154)
molded (154)	indignity (155)	leering (155)	wobbling (155)
immobilized (155)	agile (155)	mirth (156)	leisure (156)
bunched (157)	bloodlust (157)	mounting (158)	girth (158)
hollow (158)	midmotion (159)	twining (159)	exhilaration (160)
clearheaded (160)			

Discussion Questions

1. How does Mama explain to Shabanu that she will be able to survive the heat when she will not be able to eat or drink during Ramadan? Is Shabanu satisfied with the answer? *(Mama says it is a matter of faith and will. No.)*

2. Why is Shabanu worried that Phulan may not be able to manage as the wife of a hard-working farmer? *(Phulan seems to be weak, her soft hands hurt when she tries to pull the rope, and she is uncertain as to what to do.)*

3. Why does Bibi Lal wish that her husband were still alive? *(He would be so happy to see the daughters of his beloved cousin marry his sons.)*

4. Explain how the camp is made with the help of Bibi Lal and Sakina? *(Frames are made of cut tree branches and reed mats are tied against them. The roof is thatched with khip and a mud platform is made to serve as a kitchen.)*

5. What order did Dadi give Shabanu in regards to Phulan? Why? *(Dadi told her to stay with Phulan every second because Nazir Mohammad, a dangerous man, has returned from the city.)*

6. How does Phulan feel when she sees the cottage made for her and Hamir? *(She seems to be pleased. Her eyes turn damp and she is speechless.)*

7. What do the circles that Sakina paints on the house represent? *(The circles are intertwined for harmony in the family.)*

8. Why does the image of Kulsum bother Shabanu? *(Kulsum looks tired, anemic, and sad. Shabanu worries that her sister, Phulan, will become like Kulsum after she is married to Hamir.)*

9. When does Shabanu realize that she has disobeyed her father by leaving Phulan alone? *(When she is startled by a smooth deep voice from the bottom of the canal bank.)*

10. Why do Shabanu and Phulan need to escape from the quail hunters? *(The men want to take the girls with them.)*

11. How do the girls escape the trap? *(They throw their water jugs down the embankment and jump upon Xhush Dil's neck.)*

12. How do you think Dadi and Mama feel as Shabanu tells them about the hunters? *(They are fearful and worried for the girls' safety.)*

13. Why does Dadi tell Shabanu to stay off the track as they escape to Derawar? *(The hunters will not be able to follow them over the dunes in a jeep.)*

14. Why do you think Shabanu's fear has turned to excitement? *(Answers will vary.)*

Supplementary Activities

1. **Research:** Have the students research the Moslem religion. Have them answer the following questions: When was the religion established? In what country was it first practiced? Who was the principle leader of the Moslems? List at list 5 major beliefs of the Moslem religion?

2. **Critical Thinking:** The desert around Hamir and Murad has little water. Have the students brainstorm ways that scientists might be able to produce more water for the desert.

3. **Discussion:** Shabanu and Phulan are afraid of Nazir Mohammad. Have the students share a time when they were afraid. Have the students discuss the following questions: Whom can you turn to for help when you are in trouble or danger? What are some strategies a person could do to keep him- or herself safe?

Part 9—
Spin Gul, pages 161-173 and Yazman, pages 174-186

Vocabulary

Spin Gul—

palely (161)	quivering (163)	appease (163)	adolescent (163)
crabbed (164)	pewter (165)	swiveling (165)	exasperation (166)
bitumen (168)	pitch (168)	taut (169)	vision (169)
reflecting (169)	wheezing (169)	musty (172)	squirm (173)
burdens (173)			

Yazman—

scurry (175)	engrossed (175)	pelting (175)	instinctively (175)
pained (176)	unformed (176)	guarantee (176)	spite (177)
constituents (177)	shuffling (177)	rivulets (177)	apparent (177)
existence (178)	revulsion (178)	probing (179)	fragility (179)
consequences (179)	solemn (181)	adjoins (181)	tentatively (182)
blurt (182)	offense (183)	transfixed (183)	district (184)
council (184)	threatened (184)	confusion (184)	protesting (186)

Discussion Questions

1. Why doesn't Shabanu think that Dadi and Hamir will not be able to appease Nazir? (*Shabanu thinks of Shutr keena, camel vengeance. It is the way of camels and men of the desert. She fears what heavy price will have to be paid.*)

2. What does Shabanu worry about as she thinks about Dadi, Hamir, and Murad? (*She worries that he will be followed, or he will be caught before he gets away, or that Nazir will go straight to Hamir and Murad to exact a price.*)

3. Why does Shabanu feel relief and exhaustion as the Desert Rangers catch up with her and her family? (*Answers will vary.*)

4. Does Mama believe the Desert Rangers when they tell her that she is to go to Mehrabpur? Why or why not? (*No, She tells the Rangers that her husband would never ask her to go to Mehrabpur, he was to meet them at Derawar.*)

5. Why do you think Rahim, the brother of Nazir, will be able to negotiate a truce? (*Rahim is a politician and doesn't want trouble.*)

6. Why is Shabanu sent to the unfriendly village near Derawar? (*She is to try to find a midwife to ease Auntie's pain and perhaps to save her unborn baby.*)

7. Why do you think Auntie blames Shabanu for the trouble the family is in? (Answers will vary.)

8. What does Nazir Mohammad threaten to do to Murad's land? (*He says he will cut off the water and turn the land back into desert just out of spite.*)

9. Why is Shabanu upset with her sister's attitude? *(Phulan has aimed her entire existence at marrying Hamir, Shabanu wants to tell her to wake up and prepare for what will come next.)*

10. What does Shabanu begin to feel for Murad? *(She begins to think of him as a person she would like to marry.)*

11. Why do you think the women do not let Phulan or Shabanu join in the discussion? *(Answers will vary.)*

12. Do you think Hamir was wise when he challenged Nazir Mohammad? *(Answers will vary.)*

Supplementary Activities

1. **Art/Research:** Have the students research the star of Cancer. They should then illustrate the constellation of Cancer and try to recognize the picture that emerges from the pattern. Why is this set of stars called "The Crab?"

2. **Discussion:** Phulan believes that her wedding has been ruined. Have the class discuss a time when something they wanted or wanted to do was ruined. How did they feel?

3. **Writing:** Dadi and Murad are discussing a compromise with Nazir Mohammad. Have the students write solutions to this serious problem.

Part 10—
Justice, pages 187-193 and The Choice, pages 194-209

Vocabulary

Justice—

bolt (188)	smartly (188)	contented (189)	murmurs (190)
conferred (190)	lineage (191)	concentrated (193)	cherish (193)
bared (193)	reeling (193)		

The Choice—

churns (194)	rumbles (194)	sweeping (195)	starched (195)
tooled (195)	eavesdropping (195)	canter (195)	twig (196)
wearily (197)	gabbling (197)	tumbles (197)	fleeting (197)
realistic (197)	exquisite (197)	oblige (197)	mechanically (197)
snuffbox (197)	vaguely (198)	mangoes (198)	disturbing (198)
omens (198)	befell (198)	expands (198)	condolences (199)
postponed (199)	shudder (199)	accustomed (199)	superiority (199)
diminishment (199)	multiplies (200)	inscribed (200)	resultant (200)
wisps (200)	torpor (200)	pampering (200)	bolster (201)
fragrant (201)	tumeric (201)	cumin (201)	saffron (201)
unbearable (201)	unobtrusively (201)	experiments (201)	sculpted (201)
vial (201)	kohl (201)	pampered (202)	pleats (202)
formally (202)	remounts (202)	applicator (202)	miniature (202)
begrudge (202)	insured (202)	destined (203)	prompting (203)

savor (203)   uppity-uppity (205)   penniless (205)   raucous (205)
eccentric (205)   stalks (206)   outrageous (206)   insolence (207)
bolster (207)   merciless (208)   tilting (208)   profile (208)
flush (208)   rummages (208)

Discussion Questions

1. Why do you think Shabanu wants to know what Mama and the women are deciding? *(Answers will vary.)*

2. Why does Auntie's silence give Shabanu some hope? *(If the decision is one that works out well for all of them, she will be jealous and discontented. If it is not, she will crow and try to make Shabanu feel ashamed and responsible for the bad things that have happened.)*

3. How do you think Shabanu feels as she learns that Phulan is to marry Murad? *(She feels betrayed. She thinks Murad is more like herself and that she was promised to marry him. She is very upset.)*

4. Why does Shabanu fight Mama when she learns she must marry Rahim-sahib? *(She does not want to marry a man who is old enough to be her grandfather.)*

5. How does Mama soothe Shabanu when she says she cannot marry him? *(Mama says that Shabanu has six months to a year to get used to the idea.)*

6. How does Phulan feel about Shabanu marrying Rahim-sahib? *(She thinks it is a fine idea because they will be living close together and will be able to see each other almost every day.)*

7. Why does Mama slap Shabanu? *(Shabanu says that she will go live with Sharma.)*

8. Why do you think Rahim-sahib gives new houses and gifts to Shabanu and her family? *(Answers will vary.)*

9. Do you think Murad is happy to marry Phulan? *(Answers will vary.)*

10. What two things have occurred to Auntie since Shabanu's family has become wealthy? *(Her feeling of superiority has fled and she is losing weight.)*

11. How has Phulan's attitude changed as the wedding date becomes closer? *(Phulan becomes unbearable and orders everyone to do things for her.)*

12. What are the thoughts that run through Shabanu's head as the wedding approaches? *(She longs to be Phulan, because Phulan will marry her own dear Murad and Phulan is beautiful. She is lonely, fearful, and wants to be free to roam the desert.)*

13. Does Sharma think that Dadi made a good decision about Shabanu marrying Rahim-sahib? *(No, Sharma thinks that Dadi should have looked for further solutions.)*

14. How does Sharma believe that Shabanu can keep Rahim-sahib's interest? *(Shabanu must learn some of the tricks of women.)*

Supplementary Activities

1. **Discussion:** Dadi and Mama agree to let Phulan marry Murad and Shabanu marry Nazir Mohammad's brother, Rahim-sahib. Have the students pretend that they are Phulan and write her thoughts on marrying Murad.

2. **Literary Analysis:** Have the students discuss the differences and the similarities between Nazir Mohammad and Rahim-sahib. Students then make a Venn diagram that shows how the two men are alike and how they are different.

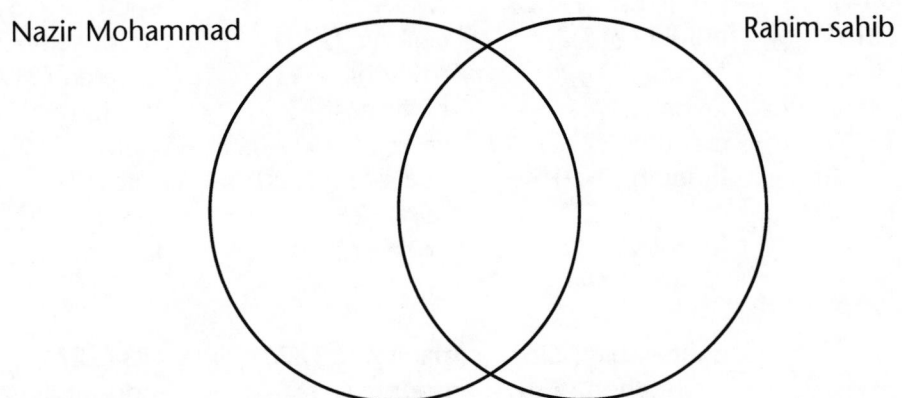

Nazir Mohammad   Rahim-sahib

3. **Critical Analysis:** Sharma tells Shabanu that she has choices. Discuss with the students the advantages and the disadvantages of marrying Rahim-sahib. Have the students record their ideas on T-charts.

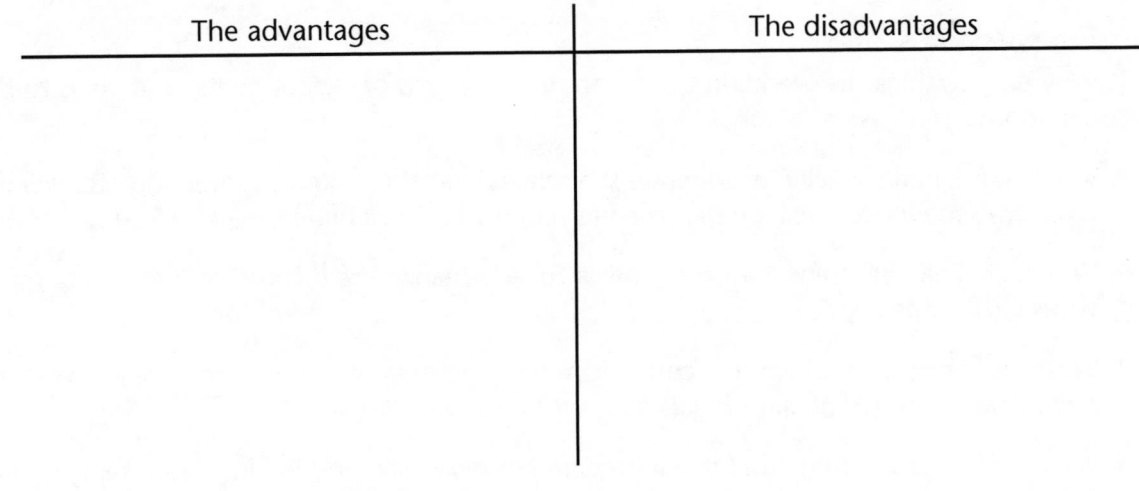

The advantages   The disadvantages

Part 11—
The Wedding, pages 210-223 and Cholistan, pages 224-240

Vocabulary

The Wedding—

humid (212)	drift (212)	haunting (213)	beckons (213)
fennel (213)	cauldrons (213)	pungent (213)	raucous (213)
throbbing (213/214)	vigil (214)	cacophony (214)	cymbals (214)
cardamom (214)	rouge (214)	tweak (215)	emerge (215)
disapproval (215)	enfold (215)	ceramic (215)	translucent (215)
scorn (216)	Mogul (216)	rhythmic (217)	flustered (217)
scanning (217)	lavish (217)	innermost (217)	partridge (217)
languidly (218)	crackling (218)	kabob (219)	churns (219)
plucks (219)	bidding (219)	quavering (220)	wafts (220)
demure (221)	cocoon (221)	nasal (221)	assent (221)
solemnized (221)	reflected (222)	hoarse (223)	discomfort (223)

Cholistan—

dapples (225)	unbearable (225)	panicking (226)	wits (227)
plips (228)	indignation (230)	pretext (231)	endure (231)
sheer (232)	defective (232)	cooperates (232)	cisterns (232)
eludes (233)	huddle (233)	thunders (233)	throttle (233)
filmy (234)	expectantly (235)	sapphire (236)	enormity (236)
expands (238)	jackals (238)	shatters (239)	vibrations (239)
haze (240)			

Discussion Questions

1. Why do you think the wedding guests bring their herds of sheep, goats, and cows to the ceremony? *(Answers may vary.)*

2. What does Shabanu tell Phulan when she relates that she is afraid something else will go wrong? *(Shabanu tells Phulan that she has had her bad luck and now everything will be fine.)*

3. Why does Shabanu think Rahim-sahib is a greedy man? *(She thinks that a man who takes four wives must be greedy.)*

4. Why have the mahendi women come from a village deep in the desert? *(They have come to paint Phulan's and Shabanu's hands and feet for the wedding.)*

5. Why does Shabanu think that it will be different when she and Rahim-sahib marry? *(She thinks that "his people will scorn us and our shoes with turned-up toes and rough cotton tunics.")*

6. What advice does Sharma give Phulan? *(Beauty holds only part of a man, and that for just so long. Keep some of yourself hidden. The secret is keeping your innermost beauty, the secrets of your soul, locked in your heart so that he must always reach out to you for it.)*

7. How does Sharma's advice affect Shabanu? *(Her words lift Shabanu's heart. She sees herself in a new light. Shabanu commits them to memory and knows that they are the perfect gift of wisdom.)*

8. Why do you think Sharma says that Shabanu will always have a choice? *(Answers will vary.)*

9. How does Shabanu feel about having to work in the house and not out in the desert with the camels? *(She does not want to give up her freedom. She likes the desert much more than housework.)*

10. Do you think Shabanu does the right thing when she runs away from home to live with Sharma? *(Answers will vary.)*

11. What feelings does Dadi have as he is beating Shabanu for running away from home? *(Answers will vary.)*

Supplementary Activities

1. **Research:** Have the students research the Koran. They should ask the following questions: What is the Koran? What date did it originate? Who wrote the Koran? What religion uses the Koran? What are five beliefs described in the Koran?

2. **Science/Health:** Obtain the spices mentioned in the book, *Shabanu* (e.g., cinnamon, cardamom, etc.). Have the students smell or taste the spices. They should vote on the spice they like the best.

3. **Critical Analysis:** There are many rituals in a Muslim wedding. Compare a Christian wedding with a Muslim wedding. Students should make a Venn diagram that shows their differences and similarities.

Christian Wedding   Muslim Wedding

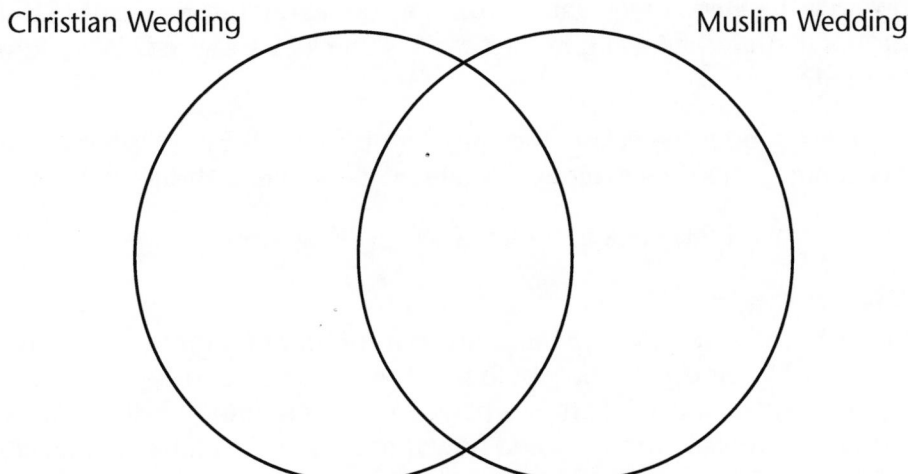

4. **Science:** Invite a vet or a doctor to talk to the class about setting broken bones. Have the doctor explain how to take care of a person or an animal who has a broken bone. The doctor may want to bring x-rays of broken bones to show the class.

Post-reading Discussion Questions, Activities and Evaluations

Post-reading Discussion Questions

1. How might things have been different if Hamir had not been killed?

2. What important lessons does Shabanu learn about Sharma?

3. As you read this story, which character did you find most appealing? Why? Which character did you find most unappealing? Why?

4. Do you think *Shabanu* is a good title for this book? Why or why not? Make up a new title for this story. Why would this be a good title for the book?

5. Have you read a story similar to this one? What is it? How is it similar? How is it different?

6. If you could change one part of this story, what would it be? Why?

7. If you had been part of Shabanu's family, would you have wanted to travel with Dadi or stay home with Mama? Why or why not?

8. How would the story have been different if it had been told by Phulan? by Shabanu's father? by Shabanu's mother?

9. The author of *Shabanu* uses humor throughout the novel. Why do you think she uses humor in a story that has the grandfather dying, Phulan's husband-to-be killed, and Shabanu betrothed to a man old enough to be her grandparent? Which scenes did you find funniest? Why?

10. Foreshadowing is the literary technique of giving clues about future events in a story. Where does the author use foreshadowing in *Shabanu*? What clues are given? What future events are being suggested?

11. What did you learn about the Pakistani culture by reading this book? What else would you like to know about the Pakistani culture? Where would you find this information?

12. Would you recommend this book to a friend? Why or why not?

Post-reading Activities

1. How do the main characters in *Shabanu* change as the story progresses? Why do the characters change? What events contribute to these changes? Choose one character from the book and complete a character chart (see page 35 in this guide) that shows how the character reacts to events in the story and how those events change the character.

2. When Grandfather is lost in the storm and becomes deathly ill, his family must decide the best way to take him to Derawar for burial. After he dies, Shabanu and Dadi search for places to bury him with honor. Have the students think of other possibilities for places to bury Grandfather. Students can use a decision-making grid (see page 36 of this guide) to evaluate their solutions and those of Grandfather's family.

3. *Shabanu* had many difficult situations to face, especially the dilemma of marrying Rahim-sahib or running away from home. Have the students think of other possibilities for solving Shabanu's problem. Students can use a decision-making grid (see page 36 of this guide) to evaluate their solutions and those of Shabanu.

4. If you could interview Suzanne Fisher Staples, the author of *Shabanu*, what questions would you ask her? Make a list of the questions.

5. If you could illustrate three scenes from this story, which scenes would you choose? Why? Illustrate one of those scenes and display your drawing in the classroom.

6. How do you wish this story had ended? Write a new ending for the book and read it to a classmate.

7. Choose a part of the story that you liked very much. Find music that expresses the feeling of the story at that point. Record that section of the story on a tape along with the background music. Add the tape to the classroom listening library.

8. Make a collage that shows important scenes from the story. You may use magazine cut-outs, drawings, and/or real objects.

9. Suppose this book is made into a film. Who would you choose to play the following roles: Shabanu, Dadi, Mama, Phulan, Sharma, Murad, Hamir, Rahim-sahib, Nazir Mohammad, Spin Gul, and Grandfather. Why would you choose these actors? Create a poster to advertise the film.

10. Make a mobile that reveals the personality of a main character from the story.

11. The theme of a story is the author's main message. What is the theme of *Shabanu*? Why do you think this is the theme? Does the book have more than one theme? If so, what are they?

Attribute Web

Directions: Put "Good Sister" in the center circle. On the spokes record descriptions. On the smaller spokes beneath each large spoke, give examples from the book or your personal experiences to support the description.

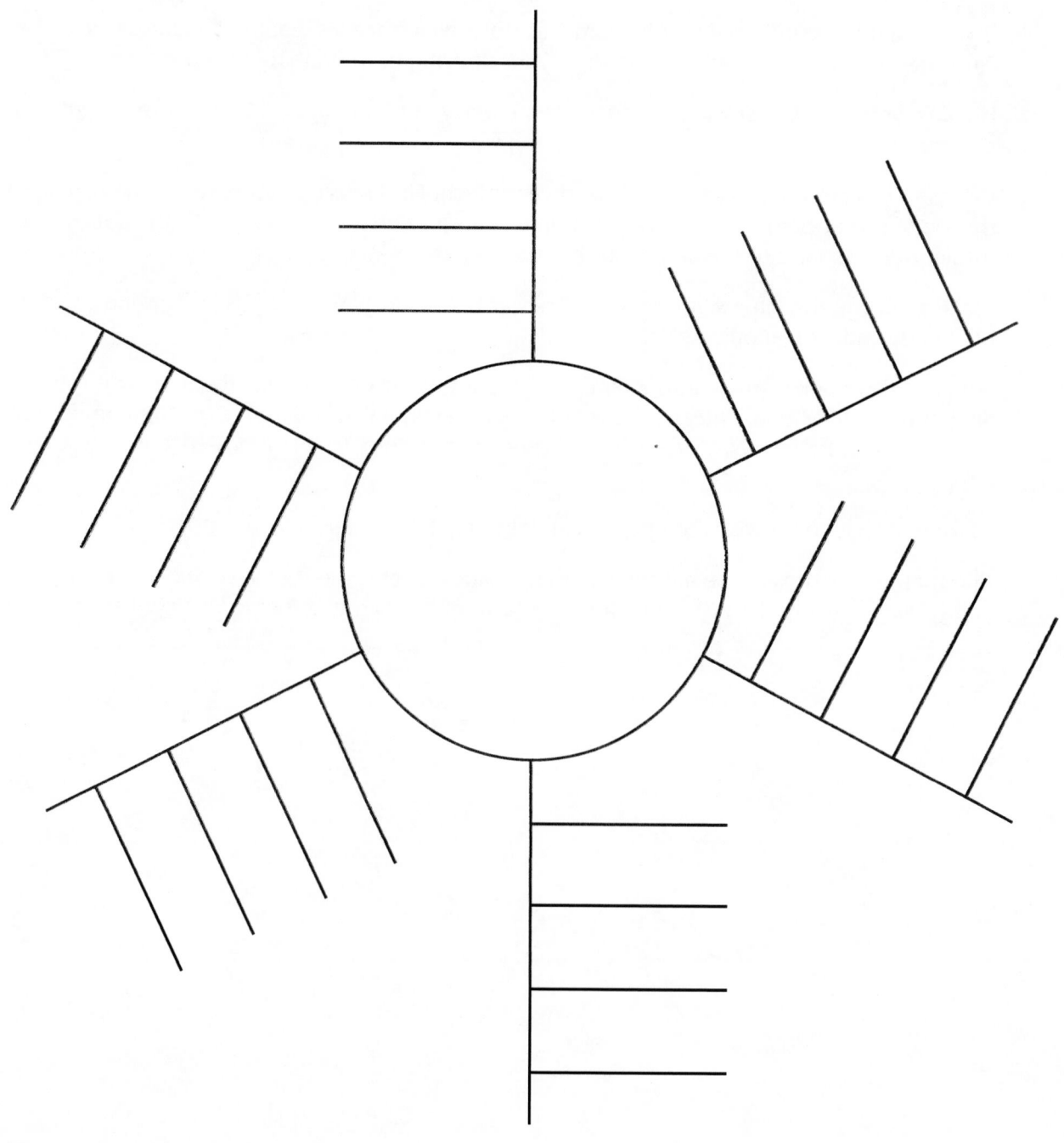

34

Character Chart

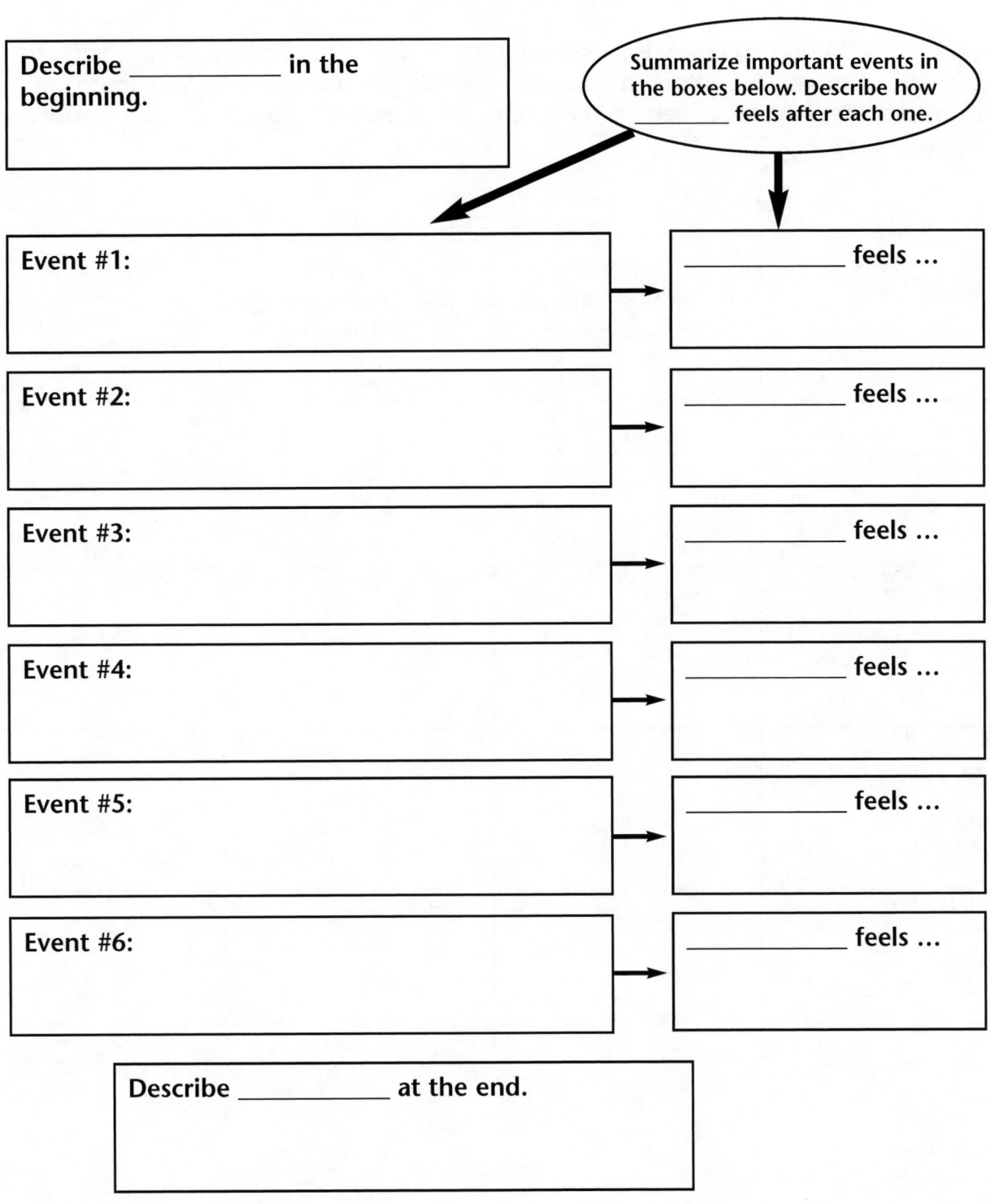

Describe _____ in the beginning.

Summarize important events in the boxes below. Describe how _____ feels after each one.

Event #1:

_____ feels ...

Event #2:

_____ feels ...

Event #3:

_____ feels ...

Event #4:

_____ feels ...

Event #5:

_____ feels ...

Event #6:

_____ feels ...

Describe _____ at the end.

Decision-making Grid

The decision-making grid below is supposed to make it easier to find the best solution to a problem. Give examples of other questions you should ask yourself when you are trying to "weigh" different solutions. Then fill in the grid. See if classmates agree with the solution you decide is best.

State the problem:	Criterion #1: Will the solution hurt someone?	Criterion #2: Will it make me feel better?	Criterion #3:
Solution #1:			
Solution #2:			
Solution #3:			
Solution #4:			

Assessment for *Shabanu*

Assessment is an on-going process. The following ten items can be completed during the novel study. Once finished, the student and teacher will check the work. Points may be added to indicate the level of understanding.

Name _____ Date _____

Student	Teacher	
_____	_____	1. Write a conversation that Shabanu might have with her father after Dadi beats her in the desert.
_____	_____	2. Research: Who are the desert people of Pakistan? What part of the country do they live in? What are their main means of making a living? What kind of foods do they eat? What types of clothes do they wear? What is their main mode of traveling? What religion are they? Name at least three of their customs that are different from your own.
_____	_____	3. List the two most important things that Sharma wanted to teach Shabanu. Explain why Sharma thought each one was important for Shabanu to know and understand.
_____	_____	4. Develop a character attribute web for Shabanu and Phulan.
_____	_____	5. List at least three humorous events or scenes from the novel. Which characters were involved in each one? Why is each one funny?
_____	_____	6. Make a chart to show the most important incidents in the novel.
_____	_____	7. Make a character collage. Cut out words and pictures from a magazine that describe one of the characters in the novel. Put the character's name in the collage.
_____	_____	8. Choose an important event from the novel. Explain how the following characters reacted to the events: Shabanu, Phulan, Dadi, Mama, and Sharma.
_____	_____	9. Write a letter to the author of *Shabanu* and tell her how you enjoyed the book.
_____	_____	10. With a partner, rewrite a scene from the novel as a skit or play, and perform it for your classmates.

Notes

Notes

Notes

40